THE TALE OF
TWO BAD MICE

BY BEATRIX POTTER

FREDERICK WARNE

ONCE upon a time there was a very beautiful doll's-house; it was red brick with white windows, and it had real muslin curtains and a front door and a chimney.

IT belonged to two Dolls called Lucinda and Jane, at least it belonged to Lucinda; but she never ordered meals.

Jane was the Cook; but she never did any cooking, because the dinner had been bought ready-made, in a box full of shavings.

THERE were two red lobsters and a ham, a fish, a pudding, and some pears and oranges.

They would not come off the plates, but they were extremely beautiful.

One morning Lucinda and Jane had gone out for a drive in the doll's perambulator. There was no one in the nursery, and it was very quiet.

PRESENTLY there was a little scuffling,
scratching noise in a corner near the fire-place,
where there was a hole under the skirting-
board.

Tom Thumb put out his head for a moment,
and then popped it in again.

Tom Thumb was a mouse.

A MINUTE afterwards, Hunca Munca, his wife, put her head out, too; and when she saw that there was no one in the nursery, she ventured out on the oilcloth under the coal-box.

THE doll's-house stood at the other side of the
fire-place. Tom Thumb and Hunca Munca went
cautiously across the hearthrug. They pushed the
front door—it was not fast.

TOM THUMB and Hunca Munca went
upstairs and peeped into the dining-room.
Then they squeaked with joy!

Such a lovely dinner was laid out upon the
table! There were tin spoons, and lead knives
and forks, and two dolly-chairs—all *so*
convenient!

TOM THUMB set to work at once to carve the ham. It was a beautiful shiny yellow, streaked with red.

The knife crumpled up and hurt him; he put his finger in his mouth.

"It is not boiled enough; it is hard. You have a try, Hunca Munca."

HUNCA MUNCA stood up in her chair, and chopped at the ham with another lead knife.

"It's as hard as the hams at the cheesemonger's," said Hunca Munca.

THE ham broke off the plate with a jerk, and rolled under the table.

"Let it alone," said Tom Thumb; "give me some fish, Hunca Munca!"

HUNCA MUNCA tried every tin spoon in turn; the fish was glued to the dish.

Then Tom Thumb lost his temper. He put the ham in the middle of the floor, and hit it with the tongs and with the shovel—bang, bang, smash, smash!

The ham flew all into pieces, for underneath the shiny paint it was made of nothing but plaster!

THEN there was no end to the rage and disappointment of Tom Thumb and Hunca Munca. They broke up the pudding, the lobsters, the pears and the oranges.

As the fish would not come off the plate, they put it into the red-hot crinkly paper fire in the kitchen; but it would not burn either.

TOM THUMB went up the kitchen chimney and looked out at the top—there was no soot.

While Tom Thumb was up the chimney, Hunca Munca had another disappintment. She found some tiny

canisters upon the dresser, labelled—Rice—Coffee—Sago—but when she turned them upside down, there was nothing inside except red and blue beads.

THEN those mice set to work to do all the mischief they could—especially Tom Thumb! He took Jane's clothes out of the chest of drawers in her bedroom, and he threw them out of the top floor window.

But Hunca Munca had a frugal mind. After pulling half the feathers out of Lucinda's bolster, she remembered that she herself was in want of a feather bed.

WITH Tom Thumb's assistance she carried the bolster downstairs, and across the hearthrug. It was difficult to squeeze the bolster into the mouse-hole; but they managed it somehow.

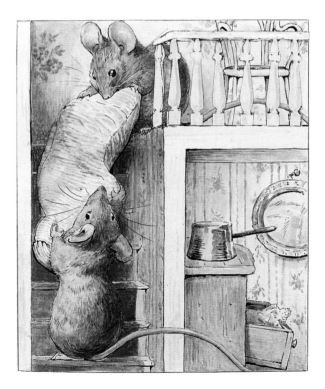

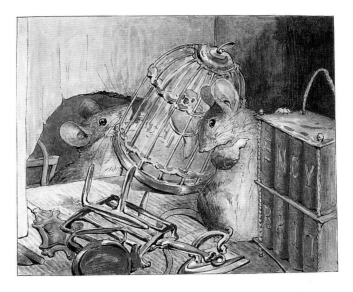

THEN Hunca Munca went back and fetched
a chair, a book-case, a bird-cage, and several
small odds and ends. The book-case and the
bird-cage refused to go into the mouse-hole.

HUNCA MUNCA left them behind the coal-box, and went to fetch a cradle.

Hunca Munca was just returning with another chair, when suddenly there was a noise of talking outside upon the landing. The mice rushed back to their hole, and the dolls came into the nursery.

WHAT a sight met the eyes of Jane and
Lucinda!

Lucinda sat upon the upset kitchen stove
and stared; and Jane leant against the kitchen
dresser and smiled—but neither of them made
any remark.

THE book-case and the bird-cage were rescued from under the coal-box—but Hunca Munca has got the cradle, and some of Lucinda's clothes.

SHE also has some useful pots and pans, and several other things.

The little girl that the doll's-house belonged to, said,—"I will get a doll dressed like a policeman!"

BUT the nurse said —"I will set a
mouse-trap!"

SO that is the story of the two Bad Mice,—but they were not so very very naughty after all, because Tom Thumb paid for everything he broke.

He found a crooked sixpence under the hearthrug; and upon Christmas Eve, he and Hunca Munca stuffed it into one of the stockings of Lucinda and Jane.

AND very early every morning—before anybody is awake—Hunca Munca comes with her dust-pan and her broom to sweep the Dollies' house!

FOR W. M. L. W.
THE LITTLE GIRL WHO HAD THE DOLL'S HOUSE

FREDERICK WARNE

Published by the Penguin Group
Registered office: 80 Strand, London, WC2R 0RL
Penguin Young Readers Group, 345 Hudson Street, New York, N.Y. 10014, USA

First published 1904 by Frederick Warne
This edition with new reproductions of Beatrix Potter's book illustrations first published 2006
This edition copyright © Frederick Warne & Co. 2006
Reissued 2016
New reproductions of Beatrix Potter's book illustrations copyright © Frederick Warne & Co. 2002
Original copyright in text and illustrations © Frederick Warne & Co., 1904

Manufactured in China

Special Markets ISBN 978-0-241-29830-5